Postman Pat® and the Big Butterflies

It was a windy day in Greendale and Julia Pottage was having trouble keeping her new hat on.

"Lovely hat, Julia!" admired Mrs Goggins. "Don't let it blow away!"

"I'd love a new hat," sighed Dorothy Thompson.

Pat was on his rounds. At the school, he caught sight of something by the side of the road.

"Look at that lovely flower, Jess. I've never noticed it before!"

As Jess went to investigate, two beautiful butterflies fluttered away.

"Miaow!"

Pat didn't notice. "Come on, Jess. We'd best be on our way."

In the classroom, Mr Pringle had some news.

"Now listen, everyone. Two very rare butterflies have gone missing from Pencaster Zoo." He held up a picture. "There's a reward of free passes into the zoo for anyone who can find them!"

The children were very excited.

"You could look for them this afternoon if you like," Mr Pringle went on, "but remember, if you find them, be gentle. Butterflies are very delicate."

Back home, Dorothy was jazzing up an old hat with some cherries from the fruit bowl. As she set off for the shops, she didn't realise that two multi-coloured butterflies had settled on her head!

"That's a pretty hat," called Pat as he drove past. "It's funny, Jess, there's something very familiar about Dorothy's hat."

The children were ready for their butterfly hunt. They crept along the road with their nets. Suddenly, Bill caught sight of a butterfly behind the hedge. "Got it!" he said, bringing his net down on top of it. But it wasn't a real butterfly – it was attached to Nikhil's buggy!

"What are you doing, Bill?" laughed Nisha.

"Ooops, sorry, Mrs Bains," gulped Bill.

Pat was trying to find the exotic flower again. "Arthur!" he called to PC Selby, who was passing by. "Come and look at this flower. It's just like the decoration on Dorothy's hat. Oh, it's gone!"

"Well I hope she didn't go and pick it," muttered PC Selby. "You're not supposed to pick wild flowers."

Meanwhile, Mrs Goggins was admiring Dorothy's hat.

"Such a pretty decoration! So many beautiful colours!"

"Well, just cherry-coloured," Dorothy replied, confused.
She still had no idea about the butterflies!

Dorothy bumped into PC Selby outside the Post Office.

"Hello, Arthur," she said. "Do you like my new hat?"

"Erm, very nice," mumbled PC Selby. "You do know you're not supposed to pick wild flowers, don't you?"

"I haven't!" Dorothy exclaimed.

"Well, what's that then?" PC Selby poked a finger at her hat, and watched in amazement as the butterflies flew away.

Dorothy took off her hat.

"It's only a bunch of cherries!" she said, baffled.

Further along the street, the children had spotted the butterflies.

"After them!"

"Don't let them get away!"

"Quick!" They ran this way and that, bumping into each other and getting into a terrible muddle. The butterflies always seemed to be out of reach.

"Hi, Dad!" called Julian, as Pat and PC Selby approached. "We're trying to catch the butterflies. They're from the zoo!"

Pat and Jess joined in as the children raced to and fro. Unfortunately, Julia Pottage got caught up in the scrum. "Good heavens!" she said, all in a spin. "Sorry, Mum!" called Tom.

PC Selby peddled his bike furiously. "Stop right there!" he called to the butterflies, as he sped down the hill. And then CRASH! His bike went into the wall and he went over it!

A little way up the road, Dorothy sat down to have a rest after all her shopping. Two exotic butterflies were heading for her hat . . .

From the other side of the wall, Pat crept up and carefully put Charlie's net down over Dorothy's head.

"Help!" she cried. "What's going on?"

"Sorry, Dorothy," said Pat. "Just stay still for a moment."

"Mum!" puffed Bill, catching up. "You've got the missing butterflies! They escaped from Pencaster Zoo!"

Pat lifted the net from Dorothy's hat, keeping the butterflies safely inside.

"Look, Dorothy, they were on your hat," Pat explained. "They must like the cherries!"

"So *that's* why Mrs Goggins said my hat was colourful," sighed Dorothy.

"We need something to put them in, so I can take them back to the zoo," said Pat.

"What about one of my new storage boxes?" suggested Dorothy.

"Perfect!" Pat made holes in the lid so the butterflies could breathe. "We'll buy you another box, Dorothy!"

"Your hat was a good butterfly-catcher, Dorothy," joked Julia Pottage.

"Yes, well, I don't think it was really me, anyway," said Dorothy, stuffing her hat in her bag and getting out her old scarf. "I like my scarf. It's more. . . practical."

At that very moment, a sudden gust of wind blew Julia's hat right off. "Oh! My hat!" she shrieked, chasing after it.

"More trouble than a butterfly!" chuckled Postman Pat, and everyone laughed.

SIMON AND SCHUSTER
First published in 2006 in Great Britain by Simon & Schuster UK Ltd
Africa House, 64-78 Kingsway
London WC2B 6AH

Postman Pat® © 2006 Woodland Animations, a division of Entertainment Rights PLC
Licensed by Entertainment Rights PLC
Original writer John Cunliffe
From the original television design by Ivor Wood
Royal Mail and Post Office imagery is used by kind permission of Royal Mail Group plc
All rights reserved

Text by Alison Ritchie © 2006 Simon & Schuster UK Ltd

A CIP catalogue record for this book is available from the British Library upon request

ISBN 1 416 91078 6

Printed in China
1 3 5 7 9 10 8 6 4 2